The Boxcar Children® Mysteries

THE GUIDE DOG MYSTERY

created by
GERTRUDE CHANDLER WARNER

Illustrated by Charles Tang

ALBERT WHITMAN & Company
Morton Grove, Illinois

Library of Congress Cataloging-in-Publication Data

Warner, Gertrude Chandler, 1890-1979
The guide dog mystery/created by Gertrude Chandler Warner;
illustrated by Charles Tang.
p.   cm. — (The boxcar children mysteries)
Summary: When they help out at a guide dog training school,
the Alden children meet several people who seem obsessed
with a particular dog named Ginger.
ISBN 0-8075-3080-8 (hardcover)
ISBN 0-8075-3081-6 (paperback)
[1. Mystery and detective stories. 2. Guide dogs-Fiction.
3. Dogs-Training-Fiction. 4. Brothers and sisters-Fiction.]
I. Tang, Charles, ill. II. Title.
III. Series: Warner, Gertrude Chandler, 1890-Boxcar children mysteries.
PZ7.W244 Gu   1996   96-6779
[Fic]-dc20   CIP
                                              AC

Cover art by David Cunningham.

Contents

THE GUIDE DOG MYSTERY

CHAPTER 1

A Special Kind of Dog

"I wish we had a mystery to solve," Benny Alden said, kicking a stone that lay in the road. Benny was six years old and liked to do exciting things, like tracking down clues and finding suspects.

Benny's sister Jessie, who was twelve, was more patient. "I'm sure something mysterious will come along."

"Something always does," added their fourteen-year-old brother, Henry.

The Aldens had reached the grocery store

in downtown Greenfield. Their grandfather's housekeeper, Mrs. McGregor, had asked them to pick up some things for dinner. The others waited while ten-year-old Violet, wearing her favorite lavender sweater, tied their dog's leash to a parking meter. "We'll just be a minute, Watch," she told him. The dog lay down on the sidewalk.

"I wish Watch could come inside with us," said Benny. "He could help pick out his favorite dog food."

Watch's ears pricked up, and he quickly stood. But it wasn't the mention of dog food that had interested him.

"What is it, boy?" asked Henry.

Watch started barking loudly. The children looked in the direction Watch was facing and saw a young man with dark curly hair coming out of the grocery store. He was walking with a dog.

"I think Watch just spotted that golden retriever," said Violet.

"I thought Jessie said dogs weren't allowed in the grocery store," said Benny.

"From the dog's harness, I'd say that's a very special kind of dog," Jessie said, as the man and dog came closer. "It looks like a guide dog."

"What's that?" asked Benny.

"It's a dog that helps blind people," Jessie explained.

"If that man can't see, then why is he wearing a blindfold over his eyes?" asked Violet.

The children took a closer look. Violet was right. The man had a rolled-up scarf tied around his head, covering his eyes.

Watch was still barking, but Jessie managed to quiet him by gently stroking his head.

The man stopped on the sidewalk and the guide dog sat down beside him. The children watched as the man removed his blindfold and spoke to a red-haired woman who had been walking behind him.

"I'm going to go pat that dog!" cried Benny, running toward the golden retriever.

Benny squatted and reached out his hand toward the dog.

"You know, you really shouldn't distract a guide dog when it's working," the man told Benny, his voice gentle. "But it's okay this time."

"What do you mean?" Benny asked, as the other Aldens came to join him.

"I'm sorry if my brother is bothering you," Henry said to the man.

"Oh, no, it's quite all right. I enjoy meeting young people who are interested in animals," said the man with the curly hair. "I'm Jason Peters." He motioned to the woman beside him. "This is Mrs. Carter. She opened the Greenfield Guide Dog School just a few years ago. I work there as an instructor. And this is Ginger." He stroked the golden retriever's back. "She's one of my students."

"She looks like a very good student," said Violet, noticing how obediently Ginger sat at Jason's feet.

"As a matter of fact, she just passed her final exam," Jason said. "She was leading me, and Mrs. Carter was walking behind to make sure Ginger did everything right."

"Is that why you were wearing a blind-fold?" asked Jessie.

"Yes," Jason said. "I had to make sure Ginger would be able to lead someone who couldn't see. Now that she's completed her training, a blind person can use Ginger to get around. They'll be able to go to stores and restaurants, ride on buses, even cross busy streets, and never have to worry."

"That's amazing," said Henry. "How did you teach Ginger to do that?"

"It takes a lot of training," Jason explained. "If you'd like to come by the school tomorrow, I'll show you how we work."

"Wow!" cried Benny.

"We'd love to!" said Jessie. "By the way, we're the Aldens. I'm Jessie, and this is Henry, Violet, and Benny."

"My goodness," said Mrs. Carter. "Are you James Alden's grandchildren?"

"Yes, we are," answered Henry.

"I went to college with your grandfather. We've been friends for years," Mrs. Carter said. "I'd hoped to someday meet the wonderful grandchildren he's always talking about."

There was a whining sound behind them, and everyone turned to see Watch, still sitting by the parking meter. He was getting restless.

"That's *our* dog," said Benny proudly, as Jessie walked over and untied Watch's leash from the meter. She led him over to meet Jason, Mrs. Carter, and Ginger. After the two dogs had sniffed each other, Jessie told Watch to sit down, and he sat quietly at her feet.

"Do you think he could become a guide dog?" asked Benny.

"He might," said Jason, smiling at Benny. "He looks like a very good dog. But our school only uses special dogs that are trained from the time they're puppies."

"I can see that you children know how to handle animals," said Mrs. Carter. "I have an idea I'd like to discuss with your grandfather."

"What is it?" asked Benny eagerly.

Mrs. Carter just smiled. "I think I'll wait and speak with him first." She looked at her watch. "Oh! I've got to run. Nice meeting you all. See you later, Jason."

As Mrs. Carter hurried off, the children wondered what her idea was. They were so thrilled about visiting the guide dog school that they almost forgot to buy the things Mrs. McGregor had asked them to get for supper!

That evening, the children could hardly wait for their grandfather to get home so they could tell him about their plans for the next day. It was almost dinnertime. They sat in the old boxcar on the lawn behind their grandfather's house and listened for his car.

The boxcar hadn't always been in that spot. It used to be in the woods. When their parents had died, the children had run away and lived in the boxcar. But then their kind grandfather had found them and brought them to live with him. They'd been very happy ever since. The only thing they'd missed was their boxcar, and so Grandfather had moved it to the backyard.

"I think I hear Grandfather's car now!" cried Benny, jumping up and running out the door of the boxcar. The other children followed.

Sure enough, Grandfather was just pulling into the garage.

"Grandfather! Grandfather!" they all cried, running up to him and giving him big hugs.

"What a nice welcome!" Mr. Alden said.

"Guess what!" said Benny. "We're going to visit a guide dog school tomorrow!"

"Are your suitcases packed?" their grandfather asked.

"We're just going for the day," Violet said.

"That's not what I hear," said Grandfather.

"What do you mean?" asked Henry.

"I got a phone call from my old friend Betsy Carter today, and she wants you to spend the week there," Grandfather explained. "There are extra rooms on the dormitory floor, where you can stay."

The children were so surprised that at first they didn't know what to say. But Benny was rarely quiet. "A whole week?" he asked.

"Yes," Grandfather said. "Betsy only has a small staff, and it seems that most of them are away on vacation, so she needs some help. If you aren't interested, I could always call her back — "

"Of course we're interested!" Jessie exclaimed. "What a week we're going to have!"

Benny's eyes lit up. "And maybe we'll even find a mystery!"

The others laughed, but they didn't realize that Benny was right.

CHAPTER 2

A Big Black Car

The following afternoon, Grandfather drove the children to the guide dog school. The Aldens looked out the window with interest as they headed up the school's long, winding driveway. A brick building sat at the top of the hill. On the beautiful green lawn in front, several people walked about with dogs.

Grandfather stopped the car in front of the main entrance and the children piled out eagerly.

"Welcome!" called Jason, who'd been watching for the Aldens. He took the suitcases from Violet and Benny's hands. "I'll take you up to your rooms."

"I have to get to work," Mr. Alden said, getting back in the car. "I'll pick you up in a week! Be on your best behavior for Mrs. Carter. She's going to look after you."

"We will, Grandfather. Good-bye!" the children called as he drove off.

Jason led the children across the wide, sunny lobby and into the elevator. He pressed the button for the fourth floor. The children noticed that along with the number, each button had small bumps on it.

"Those bumps say the number in braille," Jason explained. "Blind people feel the bumps to know which button to push." As they passed each floor, a bell rang. "If you want to know what floor you're on, you don't have to see the number. You can just count how many times the bell rings," Jason told them.

At the fourth floor, they got off the elevator and walked down a hall lined with doors, like a hotel.

"What are all these rooms for?" asked Jessie.

"Remember I told you that I teach dogs?" Jason replied. "Well, I also teach people. When someone gets a guide dog, they have to learn how to work with the dog. So they stay here for a few weeks while they're learning. We had a couple of extra rooms for you."

Jason brought them to two small but comfortable rooms, side by side. One was for Henry and Benny, the other for Violet and Jessie. Each room had two beds, dressers, desks, and chairs. They dropped off their suitcases, and then Jason continued their tour.

"This building is shaped like a U," he told them. "If you ever need me, my room is on this floor, on the other side of the U."

"You live here?" Violet asked.

"Yes," Jason explained, "because I'm responsible for the dogs day and night. It's easier to live on the campus."

The third floor held offices, including Mrs. Carter's. The dining room and lounge were on the second floor.

"But where are the dogs?" asked Benny.

"Don't worry, that's where we're headed right now!" Jason answered, as he led the children out the back door of the main lobby.

Behind the main building, surrounded by dense woods, was a smaller building with a fenced-in yard. The yard was filled with dogs: German shepherds, golden retrievers, and Labrador retrievers. Some of the dogs were sniffing about; others ran back and forth barking.

"The dogs get their exercise out here," Jason explained. "Inside there's a separate area for each dog, with the dog's food, water, and a place to sleep."

"All of these dogs are going to be guide dogs?" asked Benny.

"Most of them will," Jason said. "We start with very special puppies, who are raised by local families. In their first year, the puppies get used to being around people, traffic, and things like that. They also learn to be obedient, to follow simple commands like 'sit' and 'stay.' When they're a little over a year old, the families bring them back to the school to be trained."

"You mean they have to give the dogs back?" asked Violet. "How sad! I know I couldn't give Watch up."

"It is hard, but the families know the dogs are being trained for important jobs," Jason said.

Jason walked over to the gate. "How about if I show you one of the dogs I'm working with now?" He slipped into the yard, careful not to let any of the dogs out. He took a black Labrador by the collar and led him out to greet the Aldens.

"This is Zach," Jason said. The children sat down on the grass and stroked Zach's sleek coat. The dog rolled about on the grass playfully.

"The training takes a few months," Jason continued. "Our instructors decide whether the dogs are fit to be guide dogs. They have to be friendly, smart, obedient, and hard-working. The ones that pass the final exam, as Ginger did yesterday, are then matched with people who want a guide dog."

"Are there some dogs that fail?" asked Violet.

"Yes. Some dogs are too shy or too aggressive, or just don't follow the commands. They're given away as pets," Jason said.

"Is Zach going to be a guide dog one day?" asked Benny.

"I hope so. How would you like to watch me train him?" suggested Jason.

"That would be great!" said Henry.

Jason went into the kennel. The children noticed that Zach sat up alertly when Jason returned carrying a leather harness. "He knows when he sees the harness that it's time to stop playing and start working," Jason explained.

"They take their jobs very seriously, don't they?" said Jessie.

"They have to," Jason said. "People depend on them."

Jason let the Aldens feel the harness before he strapped it onto Zach. The straps around the dog's body were soft and comfortable, but the handle was firm, with a metal frame inside. Jason explained that a regular leash would be too loose and wouldn't allow the person and the dog to work together as well.

After he'd strapped on the harness, Jason stood up. "Come," he called to Zach, his voice firm.

Zach moved to Jason's left side and stood next to his left leg, waiting for the next command.

"Forward!" Jason said. Zach began to walk forward as Jason followed. "Notice how he walks slightly ahead of me, to lead me," Jason pointed out. "Other trained dogs are usually taught to heel, or walk slightly behind. But guide dogs need to lead their owners."

"Watch walks ahead — but usually it's because he's chasing squirrels," said Benny, and they all laughed.

"Right," Jason said to Zach, and the dog

turned to the right. "Left," Jason said, and Zach turned left.

"What a good dog!" said Violet.

Then Jason dropped a leather glove on the grass as they were walking. He walked a few more steps and then stopped. "Fetch," he said, letting go of the harness. Zach ran back and picked up the glove in his mouth. Then he came back and stood waiting at Jason's left leg.

"Good boy," Jason said, taking the glove from Zach's mouth. "Fetching is an important skill, in case a person drops something when he's out with his dog," Jason told the children. Then he turned his attention back to Zach.

"Sit!" Jason said, and Zach sat right at his feet. Then Jason said "Down!" and the dog lay down on the grass.

Jason broke into a grin. He was obviously very pleased with Zach's performance. "Good boy," Jason murmured over and over in a warm, kind voice as he rubbed Zach's head and back. "We don't reward the dogs with biscuits when they do well," he explained. "We just give them lots of praise."

The Aldens watched as Jason worked with Zach again and again on the same commands. Almost every time, Zach behaved perfectly.

One time a bird hopped across their path. Zach began to bark and chase after the bird, until Jason scolded him. Immediately, Zach returned to his position next to Jason.

"We don't punish the dogs when they misbehave, we just speak to them in an angry tone of voice," Jason said. "Soon he'll learn not to get distracted when he's working."

When Jason decided that Zach had worked hard enough, he took off the harness and led the dog back into the yard with the others. When Jason came back out, he had another dog with him.

"Hey, Ginger!" cried Benny.

"I thought you might like to say hello to her," Jason said. "Let's take her harness off now, since she's not working."

"I'll help," offered Jessie, bending over.

Benny crouched down next to Ginger, petting her back.

Ginger lay down in the grass next to the Aldens. Jessie stroked her long, golden fur, and Ginger closed her eyes. Suddenly, her eyes opened and she lifted her head.

"Ginger!" they all heard a voice calling.

Ginger got up and raced down the hillside. The children watched as a big black car pulled up at the curb, and a tall well-dressed blond woman got out. "Ginger!" she called again, opening her arms as the dog raced toward her.

"Mrs. Davis!" Jason said angrily, walking briskly down the hill. When he reached the woman, Jason began speaking to her in low tones. While they couldn't hear what the two were saying, the children could see how angry Jason looked.

"I wonder what's going on," Jessie said.

"Jason seemed so nice and friendly, but now he looks like a different person," said Violet.

The children watched in surprise as Jason

grabbed Ginger's harness and began pulling her back up the hill. "Please stop this,
Charlotte," Jason called to the woman. "I've
told you it's just not a good idea! You did
a great job with her, but she belongs here
now!"

The chauffeur of the car, a young blond
man, stared straight ahead.

Mrs. Davis stood silently. Finally she got
back in her limousine. "Take me home,
Glen," she said, and the car pulled away.

"Jason — " Benny called out as he approached.

"I'm sorry, but I have work to do now,"
Jason said, walking past the children. He still
seemed angry.

"Can we do anything — " Jessie began.

"Go eat dinner or something," Jason said.
"I'm busy." And with that he led Ginger into
the kennel and shut the door.

"I wonder what that was all about," Henry
whispered to Jessie.

"I don't know, but there's definitely something going on," Jessie replied.

CHAPTER 3

Someone Hiding in the Woods

Following Jason's suggestion, the Aldens headed to the dining room. It was a bright, pretty room, and the smells coming from the kitchen were delicious. Each table was covered with a clean white cloth and decorated with a small vase of flowers. Tonight was Taco Night, and several students and instructors were enjoying the food and lively music. The children noticed that there were also several guide dogs, each one sitting quietly under its owner's chair.

After dinner the children took a stroll around the beautiful wooded grounds and then went back to their rooms to get ready for bed.

"I hope all those dogs don't bark and wake us up the way Watch sometimes does," said Benny.

But the dogs didn't make a sound.

The next morning the Aldens ran into Jason on their way to breakfast. He was cheerful and friendly, and he seemed to have forgotten whatever had upset him the night before. After a hearty breakfast of eggs and bacon, toast, and milk, the children went outside and watched as Jason worked with Zach and some other dogs.

Around noon, the children ran into Mrs. Carter, who was walking with a girl just four years older than Henry. She was very pretty and had shiny black hair that hung almost to her waist. The girl had one hand on Mrs. Carter's arm, and in the other hand she held a suitcase.

"Hello!" Mrs. Carter greeted the Aldens. "This is Anna Chang, a student who's come to start working with a guide dog. I was just telling her about you. This is Henry, Jessie, Violet, and Benny."

Anna smiled and said hello as each Alden shook her hand.

"Would you please take Anna up to her room? It's right next to yours. Then maybe you could all have some lunch," Mrs. Carter suggested.

"Sure," said Benny. "I'm really hungry!"

"I bet I'm even hungrier!" Anna said, and everyone laughed. The Aldens knew they had found a friend.

Anna placed her hand on Henry's elbow so that he could guide her. Jessie took Anna's suitcase. Once they were in Anna's room, Anna asked how the room was laid out. Violet showed her where the bed, dresser, desk, and chair were. Anna paid close attention, placing a hand on each. She wanted to be sure she would be able to find everything later, on her own.

During lunch, Anna told the children how excited she was to be getting a guide dog. "I've been blind since I was born," Anna told them, "and I've never really felt independent. Whenever I want to go somewhere — to school or a store or a friend's house — I always have to ask someone to help me."

"I can't imagine not being able to just get on my bicycle and go wherever I want," said Benny between bites of his grilled cheese sandwich.

"It must be really hard," Violet agreed.

"I've seen blind people using canes," said Henry, taking a sip of his milk. "Have you tried that?"

"Yes, but it's hard to get around. A guide dog gives you complete freedom. I start college in the fall, and for the first time in my life I want to really be on my own." Anna smiled broadly as she thought about her future.

"Your dog will be your best friend," said Jessie.

"Yes," Anna said. But the children noticed her smile had faded a little.

"What's wrong?" asked Violet.

"Oh, it's nothing," Anna said. She picked up her ham sandwich and then put it back down on her plate. "It's just that . . . I've never had a pet before. I hope I'll know what to do."

"Don't worry," Jessie said. "I'm sure they'll teach you everything you need to know."

After lunch, the Aldens took Anna out to the kennel, where she'd been told to meet Jason.

"This is Anna Chang," Henry said when they spotted Jason.

"Nice to meet you," Jason said. "I'll be teaching you how to work with your dog."

While Jason and Anna were talking, Benny thought he heard a rustling noise in the woods behind them. He walked over to see what it was. He wondered if one of the dogs had gotten out of the yard.

Benny saw someone peering through the trees. The person was very tall and dressed in a dark suit. That's odd, Benny thought. Why would someone be walking around in the woods behind the kennels? He started to wave, but as he lifted his arm, the person ducked behind a tree, as if he or she didn't want to be seen.

"Benny!" called Henry.

"Henry, there's someone — " Benny began.

"Come on!" Jessie cried. "Anna's first lesson is starting."

Not wanting to miss anything, Benny forgot about the person in the woods and hurried over to the others.

Jason was showing Anna the dog harness that he'd shown the children the day before. She felt the leather and held it the way Jason showed her. Then Jason held the bottom of the harness and they practiced for quite a while, with Anna giving the commands he had taught her, and Jason leading her back and forth on the grass.

"Make sure your voice is firm," Jason reminded her. "The dog needs to know that you're the boss. Well, are you ready to meet your dog?"

Anna nodded, a nervous look on her face. "I guess so."

"I'll be right back," Jason said. He slipped into the exercise yard and came back out a moment later with a dog on a leash. It was Ginger!

"Here she is," he told Anna. "Her name is Ginger. She's a golden retriever with a reddish golden coat."

Anna reached out her hand and Ginger sniffed it. Then Anna cautiously put her hand on Ginger's soft back and slowly began stroking her. A warm smile spread across Anna's face.

"I think you two should have a little time by yourselves, to get to know each other," Jason said.

"We'll go stop by Mrs. Carter's office and see if she has any work for us," Jessie said.

As they turned to say good-bye to Anna, they saw her sitting on the grass, speaking softly to Ginger. It looked as if she and the dog were going to get along just fine.

"Am I glad you're here!" Mrs. Carter told the children when they entered her office. "My secretary is on vacation, and I have to run to a meeting." She quickly explained what she needed them to do: file papers, move stacks of folders, answer the phone. "I'll be back in about an hour," she said as she left.

The children set to work sorting the papers on Mrs. Carter's desk. When the phone rang, they took turns answering it and writing down the messages.

After a short while Benny noticed a shadow through the smoked glass of Mrs. Carter's door. He wondered who it was and why the person didn't just come in. Then he remembered the figure he'd seen in the woods. Could it be the same person?

At last, whoever it was knocked on the door.

"Come in," Henry called.

The door opened slowly, and a man walked in and looked around. He was wearing a dark suit with a flower on the lapel. His hair was neatly groomed and he had a little mustache. He seemed confused.

"Can we help you?" Jessie asked.

"Yes . . . uh . . . I'm looking for the director," he said at last.

"Mrs. Carter's not here right now. Can we give her a message?" Henry replied.

"That dog out on the lawn. I want to buy her," the man said.

"But — " Jessie began.

"She's a beautiful golden retriever. I simply must have her," he went on.

"I don't think she's for sale," Henry said, realizing the man must mean Ginger. "She's a guide dog."

"What do you mean she's not for sale?"

the man said. "That's ridiculous. Just tell me the price."

"I'm sorry, sir. You'll have to ask Mrs. Carter," Jessie said.

The man looked around the room at the children and drew in a deep breath. Then he turned on his heel and left, as abruptly as he'd come.

"That was strange!" Violet said when the door had shut behind the man.

"It certainly was!" Henry agreed.

"I wonder if he's the same person I saw in the woods," Benny said.

"What person in the woods?" Jessie asked.

Benny told the others what he'd seen earlier that day.

"There seem to be some strange things going on around here," Jessie said.

"Yes. Remember that scene between Jason and that woman — Mrs. Davis — yesterday?" Violet reminded them.

"I'm not sure about this," Henry said, "but I think we may have another mystery on our hands!"

CHAPTER 4

Barking Dogs

When Mrs. Carter returned, Henry told her about the strange man who'd wanted to buy Ginger.

"Well," she said, "sometimes people *do* want to buy the dogs."

As the Aldens got off the elevator on the second floor, they saw Anna on her way to the dining room. Benny ran to catch up with his new friend. Just before he reached her, she turned around and said, "Hello, Benny!"

Benny stopped in his tracks, his eyes wide.

"How did you know it was me?" he asked.

Anna smiled. "I just knew."

Benny didn't know what to say.

Anna laughed. "Besides," she said, "your shoes squeak when you run. I noticed that when I first met you."

"That's amazing!" Benny said as his sisters and brother joined him.

"Not really," Anna said. "Since I can't see, I have to be more aware of sounds and smells and other things," she explained. "I know Violet must have just come over, because I can smell her shampoo."

"Here I am," Violet said with a grin.

During a dinner of burgers and fries, Anna told them all about her afternoon and introduced them to a few of the other students she'd met that day. Anna and Ginger had gotten along very well, and the next day Jason was going to start their training together. She couldn't wait.

When they'd finished their strawberry shortcake, Anna and the Aldens went to the lounge to listen to music and talk.

At last, worn out from a busy day, the children went back to their rooms.

"I'm going to sleep well tonight!" Benny said.

But he was wrong.

A few hours later, Benny sat up in bed. He looked over at Henry, who was sleeping soundly. Benny wondered what had awakened him. In a moment he realized what it was. Outside his window the dogs were barking. They sounded upset.

Benny was just about to look out the window when he heard a soft tapping at the door. "Who is it?" he whispered.

"It's Jessie and me," he heard Violet whisper back.

Benny opened the door and the two girls hurried in.

"What's going on?" Henry asked, rubbing his eyes and sitting up.

"Something's disturbing the dogs," Jessie said.

"Or someone," said Violet, who was

standing by the window. "Come here, quick!"

The others hurried over and looked out.

"What is it?" Benny asked.

"I thought I saw someone looking in one of the kennel windows," Violet said. "But then the person disappeared."

The children all stood looking out the window as the dogs continued to bark. But all they could see was the dark kennel building.

"Maybe I imagined it," Violet said after a few moments.

The children kept watching for several more minutes, and then the dogs began to quiet down.

"If someone was there, they must be gone now," Jessie said.

"Who do you think it was?" Benny asked.

"I couldn't tell," Violet said. "Why would someone be lurking around in the middle of the night?"

"I don't know," Henry answered. "We'll ask Jason tomorrow. For now, I'm going to sleep."

*   *   *

When they asked Jason the following day, he didn't seem to think that the barking dogs were anything to worry about. "I used to wake up every time they barked, but I don't anymore. Sometimes it's a rabbit or a skunk — it's not usually anything to worry about."

"What about the person Violet saw?" Jessie asked.

"It was probably just a shadow of a tree or something. I wouldn't worry about it," Jason advised.

Then Anna arrived for her first lesson with Ginger, and the Aldens forgot all about the barking dogs. Jason told them to watch from a bench in front of the school. They had to be quiet so they wouldn't distract Anna or Ginger.

Jason put Ginger's harness on her and placed Anna's hand on the handle. While the Aldens watched, the threesome began moving down the walkway.

"Give her lots of praise, and pat her head

when she does what you want her to do,"
Jason told Anna.

Anna was nervous, and at first she almost
tripped over Ginger as they walked. But soon
she was moving slowly down the sidewalk.
Jason stayed beside them, letting Anna and
Ginger lead the way.

"Uh-oh," Benny whispered when he saw
Anna and Ginger heading toward a large
rock on the path. But Ginger led Anna
around it.

As they approached the tree-lined driveway, a large branch hung overhead. "Oh, no!
Anna's going to bump her head," Violet
whispered. Ginger could easily have walked
under the branch, but she had been trained
to notice things that might get in the way of
the person she was leading. So she carefully
led Anna around the branch.

"That's amazing!" Jessie whispered.

At the curb, Ginger stopped and waited
for Anna's command. Jason explained, "Ginger will stop at the curb, while you listen for
traffic. If it's quiet, you can tell her to go

forward. But she'll only move forward if she thinks it's safe."

"You mean she'll disobey me?" Anna asked.

"Yes," Jason said. "Guide dogs are obedient, but they're also intelligent. If a situation is dangerous — for instance, if you tell them to step out into a street with cars going by — they'll disobey you. They've been trained to think of your safety first."

Anna bent and gave Ginger a big hug. "I know I'll be safe with Ginger," she said.

The children watched the rest of Anna's lesson with great interest. It was almost time for lunch when Benny whispered to the others, "Hey, look over there." He pointed toward the road in front of the school. A big black limousine was slowly driving by.

"Mrs. Davis again!" Jessie said.

The back windows of the car were tinted, so the children couldn't see inside. They could only see her driver, who was wearing dark sunglasses, in his uniform in the front seat.

"I wonder what she's up to!" Henry said.

"I hope she's not going to interrupt Anna's lesson. Jason would be upset," Violet said.

The children watched as the limousine started to turn in the driveway.

"Oh, no! Here she comes!" said Jessie.

But at the last minute, it seemed Mrs. Davis changed her mind. There was a skidding noise as the car came abruptly to a stop. The limousine swerved back into the street. Then the engine roared and the car pulled away quickly, sending up a cloud of dust and pebbles.

Jason looked up when he heard the noise. "What was that?"

"It looked like Mrs. Davis's limousine," Henry said.

A shadow seemed to pass over Jason's face. "I think we've done enough today," he said to Anna. "Why don't you and Ginger take a break?" And with that, Jason walked quickly away.

Once again, the Aldens were left wondering what was bothering him.

CHAPTER 5

The Mysterious Visitor Returns

That afternoon, the Aldens were sitting with Ginger on the school's front lawn when a car pulled into the driveway and stopped. A man got out, and the children saw it was the same mysterious man who'd tried to buy Ginger the day before.

"Ah, just who I was looking for," he said as he walked toward the children. His voice was smooth and friendly, but the Aldens couldn't help thinking he sounded a little *too* friendly. The man reached out to stroke Gin-

ger's back, and Henry stepped away, holding her leash firmly. "If you're still interested in buying Ginger, you'll have to speak to the director of the school, Mrs. Carter."

"I should have introduced myself yesterday," the man said. He smiled broadly, but his smile seemed false. "My name's Gerard Dominick, and I just happen to be the owner of some of the greatest champion dogs in the country." He paused, waiting for the children to make some response. When they said nothing, he continued. "This golden retriever would perfectly complete my collection of dogs. I can see that she's a champion. I'll make a generous offer — "

"We told you, you have to ask Mrs. Carter," Henry repeated.

"Come, come, now," Mr. Dominick said, taking his wallet out of his pocket. "This dog is worth a fortune! Who's going to know if you just hand her over to me? You can say she ran away."

"That's terrible!" Jessie said. "You'd better leave!"

"Hey, calm down," Mr. Dominick said nervously. He put his wallet back in his pocket. "All right, all right, I'm going. But I'm not giving up!"

The Aldens watched as Mr. Dominick got back in his car and drove off.

"I don't like that man at all," Violet said.

"Neither do I," Benny agreed.

"Do you think we should tell Mrs. Carter about him?" asked Jessie.

"She didn't seem too interested yesterday," said Henry.

"Maybe we should tell Jason," Violet suggested.

The children went straight to Jason's room on the fourth floor. They were about to knock on his door when they heard his voice inside.

"It sounds as if he's on the phone," Jessie said. "Maybe we should come back later."

While the children were deciding what to do, they couldn't help overhearing what Jason was saying on the telephone. "It makes me very uncomfortable. I just don't know if it's a good idea." He paused. "All right, if you think so . . . " Jason sighed. "Okay, I'll do it."

The Aldens heard Jason hang up the phone, and a moment later, his door opened. Jason stood in the doorway, very surprised to see the children. His face turned a deep shade of red. "What are you doing here?" he asked.

"We just wanted to, um — " Jessie began.

"There's something I have to take care of," Jason said abruptly. And before they could tell him about Mr. Dominick, he was gone.

"I know it isn't right to listen to other people's conversations," said Violet as the children headed back to their rooms, "but did anyone else hear what Jason was saying on the phone?"

"Yes," said Henry. "I wonder what he was talking about. What could be making him so uncomfortable?"

"It sounds as if he's going to do something he doesn't want to do," said Jessie.

"What could it be?" asked Benny.

"And who do you think he was talking to?" asked Violet.

"Maybe it was Mrs. Davis," said Henry. "Remember the other day he told her something wasn't a good idea? He used those same words on the phone just now."

"Whatever he was talking about, he didn't seem very happy to see us on his doorstep when he came out," Jessie pointed out.

"I noticed that, too," said Violet. "He was acting *guilty* about something."

The children all thought about that for a moment. At last Benny broke the silence. "This is getting more and more mysterious!"

That night, the children ate dinner with Anna before returning to their rooms and getting into bed. They quickly fell asleep. But once again, they were awakened at midnight by the sound of barking.

"Something's bothering the dogs again," Violet said, pushing back her blankets and getting out of bed.

"I wish they would be quiet," Jessie said groggily.

Just then there was an urgent knock at the door. "Open the door! Hurry!" Benny called.

Violet went to the door and opened it. "What is it?"

Benny and Henry ran past her to the window. "Look!" Benny said, pushing aside the curtains.

Jessie and Violet followed and looked at the building opposite theirs, where the boys were pointing. All the rooms were dark.

"What are we looking at?" Violet asked.

"It better be something good or I'm going back to bed," Jessie complained.

"There!" Benny cried. A light had just appeared in the window directly across from theirs. And just as suddenly, it was gone.

"That was strange," Violet said.

"It doesn't look like light from an ordinary lamp, does it?" Henry said.

"No, it doesn't," Jessie agreed.

"Look! There it is again!" Benny called. Now the strange light was shining from a different window.

"It's moving!" said Violet.

"Why would the light be moving?" Henry asked.

"There must be someone over there with a flashlight!" cried Jessie.

"Yes! You're right," Henry said.

"But why use a flashlight inside?" asked Benny. "Why not just turn on a lamp?"

The children watched as the light went off. After several minutes, they decided that whatever had been happening there was finished. Henry pulled the curtains closed, being careful not to knock Violet's paint set off the window ledge where she had left it.

"Maybe the lightbulb burned out and the person who lives in that room has to use a flashlight," Violet said.

"I guess that's possible," Jessie said. But none of them believed it for a minute.

"I think someone was looking for something in that room. Someone who wasn't supposed to be there," said Henry.

"And he didn't turn on the overhead light because he was afraid someone would see him," Jessie finished Henry's thought.

"But someone *did* see him," Benny said. "*We* did!"

"Now we just have to figure out who it was, and what he was looking for," said Violet.

Benny yawned loudly.

"There will be plenty of time for that tomorrow," said Henry.

CHAPTER 6

A Crumpled Note

The next morning after break-
fast, the children went to the kennel to help
Jason bathe the dogs. But they were surprised to find the building locked up tight.
When they knocked on the door, there was
no answer.

"Jason must not be here yet," Henry said.

The children sat down by the front door
of the kennel to wait for him.

After several minutes, Jessie asked,

"Where do you think he is? He's usually here first thing in the morning."

"Maybe he's just running a little late," Benny said.

The children waited a few more minutes before Violet said, "I think something might be wrong."

"Let's go to his room and see if he's there," Henry suggested.

When the children got to Jason's room, he was just about to leave. He looked upset.

"Hi, Jason. Is everything okay?" Jessie asked.

"No, actually everything is *not* okay," he said angrily, letting the children into his room. "I've spent the whole morning looking for my key to the kennel and I can't find it anywhere. I was just on my way to Mrs. Carter's office to borrow hers."

"When was the last time you used your key?" Violet asked.

"Last night, around dinnertime. Then I left it in this box on my desk, like I always do." Jason lifted the top of the box so the children could see that it was empty.

"Maybe if we helped you look, we could find it," Henry suggested.

"I really need to get over there and feed the dogs," said Jason. "But if you want to stay here and look, that would be great."

"Are you sure you don't mind us going through your things?" Jessie asked.

"Not at all!" Jason said. "I've got nothing to hide."

Jessie recalled the conversation they'd overheard the day before and all the strange things that had been going on at the school, and she wondered if that was really true.

"Don't worry, we'll find it," said Violet as Jason left.

The children looked everywhere in Jason's room. Jessie looked under the bed. Violet searched the closet. Henry looked behind the chair and lamp. Benny searched the bookcase.

"Do you think it might have fallen in the wastebasket?" Benny asked, standing beside

a small basket with a few crumpled pieces of paper inside.

"Maybe," said Jessie.

Benny poked through the crumpled papers. "Hey, I think I've found something," he called out suddenly.

"The key?" asked Henry.

"No . . . but I think it's a clue," said Benny.

The others came over to see what Benny was holding. "I know you aren't supposed to read other people's letters, but this was in the trash and I couldn't help seeing what it says . . . "

"What is it, Benny?" Jessie asked.

Benny held out a crumpled piece of pink paper with the name *Charlotte Davis* printed at the top in gold letters.

Jessie took it and read the note aloud. "*Meet me tonight at eleven o'clock at Joe's Restaurant. It's important I speak to you. Please don't tell anyone.*"

"Is there a date on it?" Henry wanted to know.

"Yes. It was written yesterday," said Jessie.

"I wonder what was so important," Violet said.

"And why she didn't want him to tell anyone," said Benny.

"Do you think Jason and Mrs. Davis are plotting something?" asked Henry.

"It certainly does sound like it," Jessie said.

"Maybe that's who he was talking to yesterday on the phone," said Violet.

"We can talk about this later," Henry said. "For now, we'd better look for Jason's key."

The children resumed their search. They looked everywhere, but they didn't find the key.

"Well, I guess it's not here," said Jessie.

"We might as well go tell Jason," Henry said.

The children were taking one last look around the room when suddenly Violet ran to the window.

"What is it?" asked Benny.

"Look!" Violet said.

"All I see is the other wing of the building," said Jessie.

"That's just it!" Violet said, her voice excited. "That's the wing our rooms are in!"

"But what does that matter?" asked Jessie.

"That's our window right there!" Violet said, pointing. "See, there's my paint set on the windowsill!"

The others looked. Just as Violet said, in the window across the way they could see a paint box resting on the sill.

"That's neat! Our room is right across from Jason's!" Benny said.

"Don't you get it?" asked Violet. "Last night, when we saw the strange light, it was *here*! In this room!"

"You're right! We'd better get going, though," Henry said, "or Jason is going to wonder what's happened to us!"

The children hurried to the kennel, where Jason had already started washing the dogs.

A German shepherd stood in a large tub of water. Jason was rubbing the dog's black and tan fur with shampoo, making big soapy suds.

Jason looked up when the Aldens entered. "Did you find my key?" he asked hopefully.

"No, we didn't," Henry said.

"We looked everywhere," Jessie added.

Jason shook his head and sighed. "Thanks for trying. I can't imagine what could have happened to it. I guess I'll have a copy made from Mrs. Carter's."

"What can we do to help you with the dogs?" asked Violet.

"Cleo is ready to be rinsed," Jason said, handing Violet a hose. "Why don't you do it, and then Benny can towel her off. I hope you don't mind getting wet, Benny. Cleo usually shakes water all over me when I dry her."

"Great!" Benny said with a laugh.

Violet took the hose and began to spray the lather off of the German shepherd's back.

Cleo shook, and sprayed water all over a laughing Benny, who stood by with a fluffy white towel.

"Meanwhile, Jessie and Henry can help me get another dog started," Jason said.

Following Jason's instructions, Jessie got another large tub and began filling it with water. Henry went with Jason to get a brown dog with a smooth, glossy coat.

"What kind of dog is that?" asked Benny. "It doesn't have much fur."

"This is Ali," Jason said. "He's a boxer. Because boxers are short-haired, they can be used for people who are allergic to animals."

While Jessie and Henry washed Ali, Benny and Violet helped Jason wash another German shepherd.

Benny said as he reached for the bottle of shampoo, "What do you do at night, Jason? Do you go into town?"

Jessie gave Benny a sharp look. She knew what he was up to.

"Funny you should ask," Jason said. "Last night was unusual. I got a note from Charlotte Davis — you know, Ginger's former owner? She asked me to meet with her."

"And did you?" asked Benny.

"Benny!" Jessie scolded. "Don't be so nosy!"

A strange look passed over Jason's face. "I drove all the way to Joe's Restaurant and waited a long time, but she never showed up. It was after midnight by the time I got home."

"I wonder why she didn't show up," said Benny. But before he could say anything more, Jason changed the subject.

That night, when the Aldens sat down for dinner, Jessie turned to Benny. "I can't believe you asked Jason what he did at night!" she said.

"We wanted to find out if he'd met with Mrs. Davis, didn't we?" Benny asked.

"Yes, but . . . " Jessie began. She sighed and took a bite of her hamburger.

"But *what*?" Benny demanded.

"I think what Jessie's trying to say is that

you have to be a little more tactful," Henry explained, taking a sip of his milk.

"What does 'tactful' mean?" asked Benny.

"You have to be more careful of what you say to people, and not pry into their private lives," said Henry.

"Well, anyway, I wonder why Mrs. Davis didn't show up," Benny said. He dipped a french fry in ketchup and looked at it thoughtfully before popping it in his mouth.

"That *is* odd," said Jessie. "Especially since she said in her note that it was important."

"Remember what else Jason said? He said he didn't get home until after midnight. So he couldn't have been in his room when we saw those lights," said Violet.

"That's right! That means someone else was poking around here," Henry said. "I wonder what they were looking for."

"The key!" cried Jessie. She looked around and realized that several people at the other tables were looking over at her. "The kennel key," she said more quietly.

"But how did the person know that Jason

wouldn't be home?" asked Violet. Then her eyes lit up. "Unless — "

"Unless it was Mrs. Davis! Maybe she sent Jason that note just to get him out of his room!" Jessie said. "That would explain why she never showed up at the restaurant!"

The Aldens were all very excited about what they'd figured out. It was always fun trying to put together clues.

"But why would Mrs. Davis want the key to the kennel?" asked Violet.

"There is another possibility," said Henry. "Maybe Jason wasn't telling us the truth. He seemed very uncomfortable talking about last night, and he immediately changed the subject."

"Hey, there's Anna," said Benny. "Come join us!" he called to her.

Henry pulled over an extra chair so that Anna could sit down. Ginger lay down under Anna's chair. Violet asked how her day had been.

"It was fine," Anna said. "But I don't know . . . "

"Is something wrong?" asked Jessie.

"No — not with me," Anna said. "But during our afternoon lesson, Jason seemed to be acting strangely."

"What do you mean?" asked Henry.

"He just seemed kind of . . . nervous," Anna explained.

"I wonder why he'd be nervous," Violet said.

"Oh, never mind," said Anna. "I'm sure it's nothing."

The Aldens looked at one another. They were all thinking the same thing. Was Jason up to something?

CHAPTER 7

A Late Night for Benny

That night, the Aldens decided to keep watch out the window, to see if anything strange happened — like moving lights or fleeting shadows or barking dogs. They each agreed to take a two-hour shift while the others slept.

Benny had the first shift, from ten o'clock to midnight. While the others curled up in their beds, he sat by the window, looking out. At first it was fun staying up so late. He played cards and sipped a cup of juice and checked the window every few minutes.

But soon Benny began to feel sleepy. The room was dark, and the sound of Henry's slow, peaceful breathing made him want to crawl into his own bed. Looking out the window, he could see nothing out of the ordinary. All the windows across the way were dark. Benny knew everyone was probably asleep, just as he wished he were.

He looked at his watch. It was only eleven-thirty — he still had another half hour to go! His eyelids felt so heavy. He let out one long slow yawn, and then another. Each time he blinked, it was harder to open his eyes again.

Benny forced his eyes open wide and stared out the window, trying not to blink. But it was no use. Soon his eyes were closing again.

He didn't want to let the others down. What if something important happened and they missed it because Benny couldn't stay awake? He knew he had to do something or he would fall asleep.

Benny went into the bathroom. He turned

on the cold water and splashed some on his face. That helped a lot.

He went back to his seat by the window feeling better, but soon his eyelids were heavy again. He leaned his elbows on the windowsill and put his head in his hands. He wanted so much to put his head down — just for five minutes. What could be the harm? Benny crossed his arms on the windowsill and rested his head on top.

Suddenly he woke with a start. His arm had slipped off the sill. For a moment, he didn't know where he was. Then he remembered. He was supposed to be keeping watch. How long had he been asleep? he wondered.

Benny peered at the clock and saw that it was twelve o'clock. He smiled. It was time to wake up Henry, who was doing the next shift.

Before he woke Henry, Benny took one last peek out the window. There were no lights in the rooms across the way. He checked the kennel off to the left. And then he spotted something. From behind a tree, a shadow moved.

The shadow moved again, and this time Benny was sure he'd seen it. As if to prove this fact, the dogs began barking.

"Henry, Henry, wake up!" Benny called, his eyes glued to the window.

Henry stirred slowly. "Is it my shift already?" he asked.

"Yes, but I think I see something!"

Henry bolted out of bed and in a moment he was standing next to his brother. The two boys looked out the window.

"I saw a shadow by the kennel, and — " Benny began. "Look! There's a light moving around in the kennel! Someone's in there!"

Henry ran to get the girls while Benny kept watch.

When the girls joined them, they all agreed. It appeared that someone was snooping around in the kennel with a flashlight.

"If they're using a flashlight, I'm sure they're not supposed to be there," said Jessie.

"I bet it's the person who stole Jason's key!" cried Jessie.

"We'd better go tell somebody!" Benny said.

"Jason!" said Henry.

The children ran out of the room and all the way down the hall. They ran and ran, around two corners, to Jason's room.

"Jason! Jason! Wake up!" the Aldens called as they pounded on his door.

In a moment the door was opened by a very sleepy-looking Jason. "What is it?" he wanted to know.

"Come quickly! Someone's broken into the kennel!" Jessie said.

Jason looked confused. "What are you talking about?"

"Jason!" Henry said. "There's no time to explain. Come on!"

Jason sighed heavily. "You kids and your imaginations."

"It's not our imagination," Jessie said. "But if you don't believe us, we'll go by ourselves." The children started down the hallway.

"All right, I'm coming," Jason said, following them.

When they reached the kennel, they found the door was open, and the sound of barking dogs was deafening. As they peered into the dark building, they could see a flashlight shining down the hallway ahead of them.

Jason flicked on the overhead light, and the Aldens saw someone down the hall duck behind a large box. "Hello? Is there somebody there?" Jason called out. "Please come out at once!"

There was no response at first. Suddenly a figure darted out and began running down the hall away from them.

"He's heading for the back exit," said Jason. "I'll go around that way and try to head him off!"

The others ran down the hall after the figure. But before they could catch him, he'd run out the back exit. The heavy door slammed shut behind him.

The Aldens pushed open the door and looked out. There was a rustling in the woods. Jason stood next to the door, out of breath.

"Whoever it was, he took off into the woods before I could get to him," Jason said when he'd caught his breath.

"We'd better make sure the dogs are okay and that everything is in order," Jessie said.

The Aldens helped Jason go through the building and check each dog. Zach, Ginger, and the other dogs were all in their individual pens, just as they were supposed to be.

"Let's get back to bed," Jason said.

"Wait a minute," called Violet, who had gone back to take another peek at Ginger. "What are all these scratch marks on the gate to Ginger's pen?"

Jason came over to take a closer look. "That's odd," he said. "It looks as if someone was trying to break into her pen. There's a special latch on every pen so that the dogs can't get out. I guess the person who was in here was after Ginger." Jason twisted the

latch and opened the gate. Ginger came out and began sniffing at Jason. "Are you okay, girl?" Jason said, rubbing her back. When he was satisfied that she was unharmed, he led her back into her pen.

"What are we going to do? The person that sneaked in here probably used your key," Henry said. "He could come back."

"I'll camp out here tonight," said Jason, "and I'll talk to Mrs. Carter in the morning. We'll have to have the locks changed."

"Are you sure you'll be okay?" Violet asked.

"We'll bring you some blankets and a pillow," Jessie suggested.

"We could stay with you," Benny offered.

"No sense in all of us staying up," Jason said.

After making sure that Jason was settled for the night, the Aldens returned to their rooms.

"It's a good thing you were on watch, Benny," Jessie told her brother.

"I can't believe you were able to stay awake so late," Violet said.

"Aw, it was easy," Benny said, hiding a smile.

"I shouldn't tell you this, but we all thought you'd fall asleep for sure," Jessie said.

Benny gave her a look. "What? I can't believe you'd think that."

Violet noticed that Henry had been walking along quietly beside them. "Thinking about something, Henry?" she asked.

"What?" Henry had been deep in his own thoughts. "Oh, well . . . I was just wondering . . . did anyone else think that Jason acted strangely tonight?"

"Not really," Jessie answered. "What do you mean?"

They had reached their rooms. Jessie opened the door to the girls' room and they all went inside and sat down on the beds to talk for a moment.

"Remember when we first told him someone had broken into the kennel?" Henry asked. "He kept saying he didn't believe us, before he finally came along. I wonder if he was stalling."

"Why would he do that?" Violet asked.

"Maybe he *knew* someone was going to break into the kennel," Henry said slowly. "Maybe he wanted to make sure we didn't get there before they finished whatever it was they were up to."

"Then why did he come with us after all?" Jessie asked.

"He knew we were going, so he had to come," Henry said. "Then when we got there, remember he went around the outside to head off the person inside? He said he couldn't catch the person — but maybe he wasn't even trying."

"But he seemed so out of breath," Violet said.

"That's just it," Henry said. "I wonder if it was all an act."

"Do you think that's why he offered to keep guard?" Jessie asked.

"And he didn't want us to stay with him. . . ." Benny said.

"I can't believe Jason is up to anything bad," Violet said.

Jessie sighed. "It's possible. But we really haven't got any proof.

"Tomorrow we'll have to do more detective work."

CHAPTER 8

"Someone's Following Us!"

The next day was bright and sunny, and while eating a breakfast of fresh orange juice and waffles they saw Jason in the dining room, huddled over a cup of coffee.

"Did anything else happen last night?" Benny asked.

Jason assured them that the rest of the night had been quiet.

"It's a beautiful day out," Violet noted,

looking out one of the large dining room windows.

"Perfect for Anna's first trip downtown with Ginger," Jason said. "Let's meet in the lobby in fifteen minutes. After we walk around downtown, we'll visit Greenfield College, where Anna will be going to school in the fall. Ginger needs to get used to being on the campus with all the students."

"We've driven past the college with Grandfather," said Violet. "It's very pretty."

"I have an idea," said Henry. "Maybe we could picnic on that big green lawn."

"That sounds great!" Jason said.

"We can pick up some food while we're downtown," Benny suggested.

"I'll go to the kitchen and see if we can borrow the other things we'll need," Jessie said. She was back in a moment with a red and white checkered tablecloth, some napkins, and a knife for cutting bread and cheese and fruit.

A short while later, the group was heading downtown. The children walked a slight distance behind so they wouldn't disturb Anna and Ginger's lesson.

Jason had prepared Anna for the trip by showing her a special map of town. The streets were marked with raised lines so that she could feel where they were. He had also asked her which stores she usually visited, so that she and Ginger could practice going in those.

"We're on Main Street now," Jason told her. "Let's walk to the pet shop on the corner of Spruce and Elm. That's a place you and Ginger will be going to often."

"That's where we buy things for Watch!" said Benny.

They all began walking. When they reached the first corner, Ginger stopped right at the curb.

"Good girl," Anna said.

"Listen for the traffic," Jason told Anna.

A couple of cars went by.

"It sounds quiet now," Anna said.

"Then tell Ginger to move ahead," Jason said.

"Forward," Anna said, and they all crossed the street.

At each corner Ginger would stop and wait for Anna to listen for the traffic and decide which way she wanted to go.

When they reached the pet shop, Jason showed Anna how to enter the store with Ginger.

As the Aldens paused outside, Benny moved closer to his sisters and brother and whispered, "I think someone's following us."

"You do?" Jessie asked. She looked behind them. The only person she saw nearby was a tall figure in a long raincoat and hat. The person was standing at a pay phone making a call. Jessie couldn't tell if it was a man or a woman. "Do you mean that person on the phone?"

"That's the one," Benny said. "I noticed him as soon as we got into town, and he's been with us this whole way."

"Are you sure?" Henry asked.

"Yes," said Benny.

"Now that you mention it, there is some-

thing odd about him," Violet said. "Why is he wearing a raincoat and hat on this beautiful, sunny day?"

"Look at the way he's standing," Jessie pointed out. "Head down, hat pulled low, back toward us — as if he doesn't want to be seen."

"Or recognized," Henry added.

"Who do you think it might be?" asked Violet.

"I don't know," said Benny. "Maybe Mr. Dominick. He's tall and thin."

"So is Mrs. Davis," said Jessie. "It could be a woman, you know. You really can't tell."

"We'll keep an eye on him — or her," said Henry.

A few minutes later, Anna, Jason, and Ginger came out of the shop. Anna was carrying a small paper bag. "Look what I got," she told the Aldens.

They crowded around as she pulled something out of the paper bag. It was a new collar for Ginger, made of soft brown leather.

"She's been wearing the same collar since she was a puppy," Jason said.

"The leather is all lumpy and cracked," Anna added.

"I think she'll really like the new one," Violet said.

"I'll put it on her tonight when we get home," Anna said, as she and the others began walking.

When they'd gone a few blocks, Jessie took a quick peek over her shoulder. The mysterious person was close behind them. Each time one of the Aldens looked back, the person would duck into a doorway or pause on a corner. But he — or she — never gave up.

The next stop was the grocery store. The Aldens followed Jason, Anna, and Ginger inside.

"Let's get some things for our picnic," Jessie said, picking up a basket.

First Ginger led Anna up the produce aisle. Just like outside, Ginger was a good guide. She carefully led Anna around a display of watermelons in the center of the aisle.

Henry picked out some ripe peaches and plums and put them in Jessie's basket. Violet selected a juicy tomato. Benny got a plastic bag and filled it with dried pineapple, raisins, and nuts, which he scooped from a large bin.

Next they came to the dairy case, where Violet picked out a piece of sharp cheddar and some Swiss cheese.

When they reached the dog food aisle, Ginger began to sniff at some of the bags of dried food on the shelves. "Ginger!" Jason scolded. Ginger quickly returned to the center of the aisle. "Good girl," Jason said.

Along the back wall was a bakery, where Jessie chose a long loaf of crusty bread. Benny picked out a carton of fruit punch.

"Now all we need are paper plates and cups," said Violet as she took some off of a shelf and put them in Jessie's basket. At last their picnic was complete.

As they were standing in line at the check-out counter, Henry noticed someone moving up the aisle behind Anna and Ginger. It was the same mysterious person who'd been following them. For the first time, Henry also noticed that the person walked with a limp. "Jessie!" Henry whispered. "There he — or she — is again! I'm going after him."

Henry set off to try to get a closer look. The person was following Anna and Ginger up the soap aisle when Henry called out, "Hey, you! In the raincoat!" The person quickly darted down the canned vegetable aisle, with Henry in pursuit, but he was able to outrun Henry. As Henry raced to the end of the aisle, the person ran out the front door.

Breathless, Henry returned to his sisters and brother, who had paid for their groceries.

"Well?" Jessie asked. "Could you see who it was?"

"No," Henry said, catching his breath. "He — or she — was too fast for me."

In a few minutes, Jason, Anna, and Ginger joined them at the front of the store. "What was going on back there, Henry?" Jason asked. "Why did you run past us?"

Henry was about to answer when Anna

interrupted. "Were you after that person who was following us?" she asked.

"Yes — you knew someone was following you?" Henry asked.

"I had heard footsteps behind me for several minutes. At first I thought it was just a coincidence, but it was always the same person," Anna said.

"How do you know?" Violet asked.

"I recognized the way he walked — with a slight limp," Anna explained. "He stopped and started whenever I did."

"Did you see who it was?" Jason asked Henry.

"No, he ran away too fast." Henry looked disappointed.

"So you don't know if it was the same person who was in the kennel last night?" Jason asked.

"No," said Henry. "Could you tell if it was him, Benny?"

"No," said Benny. "I couldn't see him."

"Wait a minute. What are you talking about?" Anna wanted to know. No one had told her what had happened the night before. They didn't want to upset her.

"Well?" Anna demanded.

"We'll tell you about it over lunch," Jessie said.

CHAPTER 9

Ginger's Been Kidnapped!

Greenfield College was only a few blocks from downtown. Anna, Ginger, and Jason led the way, with the Aldens following. Jessie and Henry each carried a bag of groceries.

When they reached the college, they saw several big stone buildings, covered in ivy, around a large green lawn. Students carrying books and notebooks walked from one building to another. Some students sat on the grass eating lunch and chatting. On one side of the lawn, a couple of people were throwing a football.

Henry spotted a shady corner surrounded on two sides by tall bushes. "How about if we sit over there?" The others nodded and followed him across the lawn, being careful not to get in the way of the ball players.

Jessie got out the checkered tablecloth and spread it on the grass. Everyone sat down, and Ginger lay on the grass next to Anna. Violet placed a paper plate and cup in front of each person, and Benny handed everyone a napkin.

"What's for lunch?" Jason asked as Henry began to reach into one of the bags.

"Bread and cheese and fruit," Henry said. He placed all the food in the center of the tablecloth where everyone could reach. Jason tore off a hunk of bread and handed the loaf to Anna, who did the same.

Jessie cut the cheese into chunks and sliced the tomato with the knife she'd borrowed from the school's kitchen. Violet filled all the cups with punch.

For a moment everyone was silent, eating sandwiches of the bread and cheese and tomato. They scooped up handfuls of the dried fruit and nuts. At last, as they sat back enjoying the juicy peaches and plums, Anna asked the question that had been on all their minds. "Now, who was in the kennel last night?"

"That's just it — we don't know," Henry said. "Someone broke in — Benny spotted the person from our window. We went and woke up Jason, and then we all ran down to the kennel."

Jason picked up the story. "But when we got there, whoever was inside ran into the woods."

"What time did all this happen?" Anna asked.

"Around midnight," said Violet.

"What were you doing looking out the window at midnight, Benny?" Anna wanted to know.

"I was keeping watch. It was my shift," Benny explained.

"What do you mean, you were 'keeping watch'?" asked Jason.

The Aldens looked at one another. They hadn't really planned on telling anyone about all the strange things that had been happening at the school — at least not until they had some answers. They weren't even sure they could trust Jason. He might be involved somehow.

"Why were you keeping watch?" Anna said.

Benny looked to Jessie for help.

"Well," Jessie began slowly, "ever since we came to the school, we've noticed some strange things have been happening. The very first day Benny saw someone lurking in the bushes behind the kennel."

"Then there was this man, Mr. Dominick, who kept coming by trying to buy Ginger," Violet continued.

"*My* Ginger?" Anna put her arms around Ginger possessively. Jessie smiled, thinking how close Anna and the dog had become.

"The school doesn't sell dogs," said Jason.

"We told him we didn't think the school sold their guide dogs, but he wouldn't give up," Violet said.

"I still don't understand why you were keeping watch," Anna said.

"Does it have to do with that night you thought you saw someone lurking around the kennel?" Jason asked.

"Yes," said Benny. "And the night before last we saw some weird lights."

"Weird lights?" Jason repeated. "Where?"

"They were, um . . . " Benny paused, not sure what to say.

"Actually, Jason, they were in your room," Henry finished for his little brother. "We think someone was in there with a flashlight. And the next day, your key to the kennel was gone."

Jason sat back on the blanket, trying to take in what the Aldens had just told him. "This gets stranger all the time," he said at last. "Why would someone want to break into the kennel? Do they want one of the dogs?"

"Well," Anna said, "they're worth more than gold to people like me." She stroked Ginger's back.

"That reminds me," said Henry. "The latch on Ginger's pen was all scratched up last night. Remember?"

"And Mr. Dominick said something about Ginger being worth a lot of money — that she looked like a champion dog," added Jessie.

Anna sat up straight. "Do you think someone — Mr. Dominick — is trying to steal Ginger?"

"Could be," said Henry.

"I'm not going to let that happen," Anna said fiercely. "I'd feel safer if Ginger slept in my room tonight."

"That's usually not allowed at this point —" Jason began.

"I think it's a great idea," said Jessie, and the others nodded and looked at Jason expectantly.

"All right, but only because this is a special situation," Jason said.

After they were done eating, the children gathered up the garbage and threw it in a nearby trash can. Anna and Jason folded the tablecloth. Then they spent the rest of the sunny afternoon playing in the grass with Ginger. They were having so much fun that none of them noticed the tall person in the raincoat slinking away through the bushes.

After dinner, Anna brought Ginger back to her room instead of to the kennel. Each of the Aldens gave Ginger a pat on the head as they said good night.

"Her new collar is very nice," Violet said.

"I hope Ginger likes it, too!" Anna said with a smile. "Good night!"

The nights before had been very exciting. For a change, the Aldens were hoping they could get a good night's sleep.

But once again, something woke them. This time it was someone banging on the door.

"Jessie! Violet!" a voice called. "Wake up!"

Violet jumped out of bed and ran to the

door when she recognized Anna's voice. "Anna, what is it?" Violet asked.

"It's Ginger! She's been kidnapped!" Anna cried.

"What do you mean?" demanded Jessie.

"Someone broke into my room and took her!" Anna said.

Henry and Benny had just stumbled sleepily out of their room to find out what was going on. As soon as they heard what Anna was saying, Henry took off down the hall. "I'm going to get Jason," he called over his shoulder.

When Henry returned with Jason, Anna was sitting on her bed, wiping tears from her eyes. Jessie had gotten her a glass of water and Violet was sitting beside her, patting her hand. Benny was pacing restlessly back and forth.

"Tell us exactly what happened," Jason said.

"I was in bed," Anna began. "Ginger was sleeping on the floor next to the chair. I heard a scraping noise at my door — now I realize it must have been someone picking the lock. I heard the door open, and someone called Ginger's name. I thought I was dreaming. But when I heard the door click shut, I knew it wasn't a dream. Ginger was gone!"

"Then what did you do?" asked Jason.

"I ran out into the hallway and banged on Jessie and Violet's door," Anna said.

"When you opened the door, did you see anyone in the hallway?" Jason asked the girls.

"No. There was no one but Anna," Violet said.

"I know who the person was," Anna said.

"You do?" Jessie said.

"Oh, I don't know the person's name, but I know it was the same person who was following us today," Anna said.

"How can you be sure?" Henry asked. He noticed Ginger's old collar lying on Anna's desk and picked it up.

"I heard the way he ran. It was the same limp I'd heard earlier today, behind me," Anna said. "I also noticed that he smelled flowery — like aftershave or perfume."

"The person must have overheard us saying that Ginger was going to spend the night in your room," Violet said.

"I can't believe Ginger would just go off with a stranger," Jessie pointed out.

"Maybe it wasn't a stranger," said Benny. "Maybe it was Mrs. Davis."

Everyone looked at Benny. He could be right. The children all remembered the way Ginger had run eagerly to her former owner only a few days before.

As they were talking, Henry had been idly playing with Ginger's old collar. It seemed awfully lumpy. He noticed a small slit in the leather and slipped his finger in. All of a sudden, Henry called out, "Oh, my gosh! Look at this! There's something inside Ginger's collar!"

Everyone stopped talking and looked over. "What is it, Henry?" Jason asked.

Henry was pulling something out from inside the two layers of leather. It looked sparkly. At last he got the object out and held it up in the light where it glittered.

"It's a diamond bracelet!" Jessie cried. Everyone crowded around Henry to examine the valuable piece of jewelry.

"What was this doing inside Ginger's collar?" asked Anna, as she fingered the narrow bracelet.

"Why would someone tuck a diamond bracelet inside a dog's collar?" asked Violet.

"Oh, my goodness!" Jessie cried out. "Maybe the person who kidnapped Ginger wasn't after *Ginger* at all. Maybe the person knew the bracelet was in Ginger's collar, and that's what he was after!"

"You may be right," said Jason. "I think I'd better make a few phone calls." He picked up the phone, dialed, and began speaking quietly.

While Jason talked, the Aldens comforted Anna, who was quite upset.

"Don't worry, we'll solve this mystery and get Ginger back," Violet assured her.

"You don't know us very well yet, but we're good at solving mysteries," Benny added.

When Jason had hung up the phone, Henry asked if he'd spoken with the police. "No," Jason said. "I called Mrs. Carter. She wants to wait until tomorrow before we call the police. She's hoping we can figure out what happened to Ginger and where this bracelet came from. If we call in the police, it will be terrible publicity for the school, and we don't want that." The others all nodded.

"I called Charlotte, too," Jason went on. "She seemed very upset when I told her what happened to Ginger."

"Do you believe her?" Henry asked.

Jason looked thoughtful. "I guess so. She's going to come by tomorrow morning, and we can talk to her some more and show her the bracelet."

"Until then, I guess there's nothing more we can do," Jessie said.

CHAPTER 10

Lots of Surprises

The following morning, the Aldens woke and dressed quietly. They were all wondering what had happened to Ginger and feeling very sorry for Anna.

"I have an idea," said Violet. "Let's get some flowers for Anna. They won't take Ginger's place, but they might make her feel a little better."

"The flower shop downtown is open early," said Jessie. "We could go right now."

In no time the Aldens were walking down

Main Street toward the flower shop. Suddenly, up ahead, they saw a tall person walking a golden retriever!

It was Mr. Dominick!

"Hey, you!" Benny cried out, breaking into a run. "Stop!"

The others chased after Benny, expecting Mr. Dominick to run away. But surprisingly, he came toward them.

"Well, hello," he called out, a broad grin on his face.

"You kidnapped Ginger!" Benny shouted angrily.

But as he got closer, Benny stopped in his tracks. The others stopped right behind him. The dog wasn't Ginger! It was a different golden retriever!

"Meet Lola," Mr. Dominick said. "When I realized I couldn't get Ginger, I searched all over and found a breeder who sold me this beautiful dog. I told you I wouldn't give up."

"But we thought you meant —" Jessie began.

"You thought I meant what?" asked Mr. Dominick.

"Oh, nothing," Jessie said, patting Lola on the head. "She is a beautiful dog."

"Her first show is in two months. Come see her win," Mr. Dominick said. "Bye-bye!"

The Aldens watched as Mr. Dominick and Lola walked off down the street. "Well, I guess Mr. Dominick wasn't the one trying to take Ginger," said Violet.

"Who could it be?" wondered Jessie.

Then they turned slowly and went into the flower shop. There they selected a pretty bunch of nice-smelling flowers that they thought Anna would like, and headed back to the school.

As the Aldens were walking up the school's driveway, they saw Jason walking just ahead of them. "Hey, wait for us!" Henry called out.

When Jason turned, the children noticed he had a strange look on his face. He was carrying something in a bag, which he quickly tucked behind his back.

"So you had some things to do this morning, too," said Jessie.

"Uh, yes," Jason said. He sounded uncomfortable.

"What's in the bag?" asked Benny.

"Nothing. . . ." Jason said. He seemed relieved when a car pulled into the driveway, interrupting their conversation. It was Charlotte Davis.

A few moments later they were all gathered in Mrs. Carter's office, along with Anna and Mrs. Carter. Jason showed the diamond bracelet to Mrs. Davis. "This was tucked inside Ginger's collar. Do you recognize it?"

"I think so," she said, taking the delicate piece of jewelry from him. "It looks like the heirloom bracelet that I haven't been able to find for a few months. I'll put on my glasses and then I'll know for sure." Mrs. Davis began patting her pockets, feeling for her glasses. "Now where did I put them?" she mumbled to herself. "Oh, I must have left them in the car."

"Can I run down and get them?" Henry offered.

"Thanks, but I'll just call down to my driver to bring them up." Mrs. Davis went to the window and called down to her car, which was parked just below. "Glen! Would you please bring my glasses? I think they're in the backseat."

A few minutes later, a tall man entered the room carrying an eyeglass case. As he crossed the floor to where Mrs. Davis was sitting, Benny gasped.

"What is it, Benny?" Jessie asked.

"It's him!" Benny said. "He's the one who was following us! I can tell by the way he walks."

Glen was walking with a limp. He stopped in the middle of the room and looked at Benny.

"Are you sure?" Jason asked.

"*I'm* sure," said Anna. Everyone turned to look at Anna, who'd been sitting quietly in the corner. "I recognize the sound of his walk

from the grocery store yesterday. And I can smell his aftershave — it's the same as last night."

Glen looked around nervously.

"You think Glen is the one who kidnapped Ginger?" asked Mrs. Davis.

"Why would I —" Glen said.

Just then, the door was pushed open and someone else came into the room. It was Ginger! Trailing from her collar was a broken piece of rope. Ginger ran around the room excitedly, her tail wagging wildly. Then she raced over to Anna.

In all the commotion, Glen forgot that the others were there. "Ginger! How did you get free?" he said, not realizing the others were listening.

"So it *was* you," said Mrs. Davis.

Glen realized it was over. He hung his head sadly and said, "Yes, I admit it, Mrs. Davis. I kidnapped Ginger and tied her up in my sister's backyard. It's just down the street from here."

"But why?" asked Violet. "Why would you do such a thing?"

"It was because of the bracelet, wasn't it?" said Henry.

"Yes," Glen said. He began speaking slowly. "I thought if I stole that bracelet I'd have all the money I'd ever need. I used to take Ginger for walks every day. So one day, when we were leaving, I sneaked into Mrs. Davis's room and took the bracelet."

"How did it end up in Ginger's collar?" Jessie asked.

"After I'd taken it, I saw Mrs. Davis coming. I panicked. I didn't want her to catch me with the bracelet! So I made a slit in Ginger's collar and hid it there." He sighed. "But I didn't know that the next day Ginger was being returned to the school for training."

"So all this time you've been following us and sneaking around, trying to get the bracelet back," said Jessie.

"Yes," Glen said.

"And you stole Jason's key and broke into the kennel," said Henry.

Glen nodded. "I wrote Jason a note and signed Mrs. Davis's name. I knew that he'd go meet with her and that would give me time to break into his room and find the key."

"So that's why you never showed up that night," Jason said to Mrs. Davis. "I knew you were upset about having to return Ginger. Oh, Charlotte. I thought you were going to ask for her back. I was going to tell you I couldn't do that."

"You kept telling me not to come back and see her again, but I missed her," Mrs. Davis said.

"She needed to become attached to Anna, and she couldn't do that if you kept coming back," Jason explained. "I was afraid that you were the one who'd been following us."

"And the one who kidnapped her?" Mrs. Davis smiled. "I would never have gone that far."

While they were talking, Mrs. Carter had

gone to the phone and quietly made a call. In a few minutes, the police appeared in the doorway.

"Jason, why don't you take Anna and the Aldens outside," Mrs. Carter suggested. "We'll handle this from here."

As they left Mrs. Carter's office, Jessie turned to the others. "At last the mystery is solved!"

"It's great that we can go for a walk now and not worry someone's following us," Violet added.

"I don't know about you guys, but solving a mystery always makes me hungry," said Benny.

"Oh, Benny," said Henry. "Everything makes you hungry."

"Well, I'm hungry, too," said Anna.

"How about a special celebration at the pancake house downtown," Jason suggested.

"Good idea!" Violet said.

A short while later, Jason, Anna, and the Aldens were all sitting around a big table enjoying stacks of delicious blueberry pancakes. Ginger sat happily under Anna's chair.

"There is still one thing I'm wondering about," Benny said. "What's in that bag you've been carrying around since this morning, Jason?"

Jason's face flushed. "Well, I might as well get this over with." He reached into the bag and pulled out a single red rose. "This is for you, Anna. I wasn't sure if this was a good idea, but . . . oh, what the heck. I'm hoping that maybe when we're done with your training . . . um . . . you and I could go out, you know, on a date."

Anna broke into a smile. "I'd like that very much."

Violet grinned. "So that's what was making you so nervous!"

"And that's what we overheard that day on the phone," Henry said.

"I was afraid you might have heard me when I came out of my room that day and saw you on my doorstep! That's why I took off so quickly. I was embarrassed," Jason said. "I'd been talking to my brother about Anna. I was afraid to ask her out, but he said I should."

"I'm glad you did," Anna said, taking his hand.

At last all the mysteries had been solved.

A few weeks later, Henry, Jessie, Violet, and Benny were in the pet shop in Greenfield when they saw a tall woman standing at the counter. Beside her was a golden retriever.

"Mrs. Davis?" said Jessie.

"Hello!" Mrs. Davis said. "This is Max. I had such a wonderful experience with Ginger that I decided to train another puppy for the school."

Just then Max began yipping excitedly. The Aldens turned to see that Anna had just entered the shop with Ginger. They moved smoothly together, like a team.

"Anna!" cried Benny.

"Hello, Benny," said Anna, walking over with a big smile on her face.

"Are you done with your training?" asked Henry.

"Yes. Ginger and I go everywhere together now. It's wonderful! My whole life has changed," said Anna. "She's even coming with Jason and me to a concert tonight."

Anna knelt down and Ginger turned and licked her face eagerly. Anna laughed out loud.

"It's good to know that everyone's happy," Violet said, stroking Ginger's back.

"Especially Ginger," said Benny. "She's a very special dog."

GERTRUDE CHANDLER WARNER discovered when she was teaching that many readers who like an exciting story could find no books that were both easy and fun to read. She decided to try to meet this need, and her first book, *The Boxcar Children*, quickly proved she had succeeded.

Miss Warner drew on her own experiences to write the mystery. As a child she spent hours watching trains go by on the tracks opposite her family home. She often dreamed about what it would be like to set up housekeeping in a caboose or freight car — the situation the Alden children find themselves in.

When Miss Warner received requests for more adventures involving Henry, Jessie, Violet, and Benny Alden, she began additional stories. In each, she chose a special setting and introduced unusual or eccentric characters who liked the unpredictable.

While the mystery element is central to each of Miss Warner's books, she never thought of them as strictly juvenile mysteries. She liked to stress the Aldens' independence and resourcefulness and their solid New England devotion to using up and making do. The Aldens go about most of their adventures with as little adult supervision as possible—something else that delights young readers.

Miss Warner lived in Putnam, Connecticut, until her death in 1979. During her lifetime, she received hundreds of letters from girls and boys telling her how much they liked her books.